Joe and Chris are friends. They live by the sea. They are going to spend the day exploring on the beach at Windy Bay.

Joe is looking for shells on the beach. Chris is exploring the rockpools. They use their walkie-talkies to talk to each other.

'Come in, Joe,' says Chris.

'What's up, Chris?' asks Joe.

RESCUE AT THE BEACH

by Cheryl Brown

B⬚XTREE

First published in the UK 1993 by BOXTREE LTD, Broadwall House, 21 Broadwall,
London SE1 9PL
1 3 5 7 9 10 8 6 4 2
Copyright © 1993 ITC ENTERTAINMENT GROUP LTD.
Licensed by Copyright Promotions Ltd.
Design and illustrations by Arkadia
1-85283-562 1

Printed in Scotland by Cambus Litho Ltd.

A catalogue record for this book is available from the British Library

'Come and see what I've found,' answers Chris.

'I'll be right there,' says Joe and he runs across the beach to the rocks.

Joe climbs the rocks. Chris has found a crab in the rockpool. Joe looks in another pool and finds a starfish.

Joe and Chris are so busy looking in the rockpools they do not notice that the sea is getting closer and closer. The tide is coming in. Soon the rocks are surrounded by sea.

'What shall we do?' asks Chris. 'The rocks are cut off by the sea.'
'If we can't climb down,' says Joe, 'we will have to climb up.'
Joe and Chris climb up the rocks to a small cave at the bottom

of the cliff above them. The cliff is too steep to climb.

'Now what?' asks Chris.

'I'll use my walkie-talkie to call for help,' says Joe. 'If we are lucky someone will hear us.'

Joe and Chris are very lucky. John Tracy, the pilot of International Rescue's space station, Thunderbird 5, hears them.
John contacts his father on Tracy Island at once.

'Come in, Father. I have picked up a call for help from two boys.
They are trapped on the rocks at Windy Bay.'

'This is a job for Thunderbird 1,' says Jeff. 'You must lift the boys off the rocks before the sea reaches them.'

'OK, Father,' says Scott, 'I'm on my way.'
A minute later Thunderbird 1 is launched.

Back at Windy Bay the water is still rising up the rocks and it has begun to rain. Joe and Chris are sheltering in the cave.

'Look,' says Chris, pointing to the sky, 'it's a plane... no, it's a rocket... no, it's... '

    'Thunderbird 1!' shouts Joe.

Scott spots the boys just as some rocks fall down the cliff, trapping them in the cave.

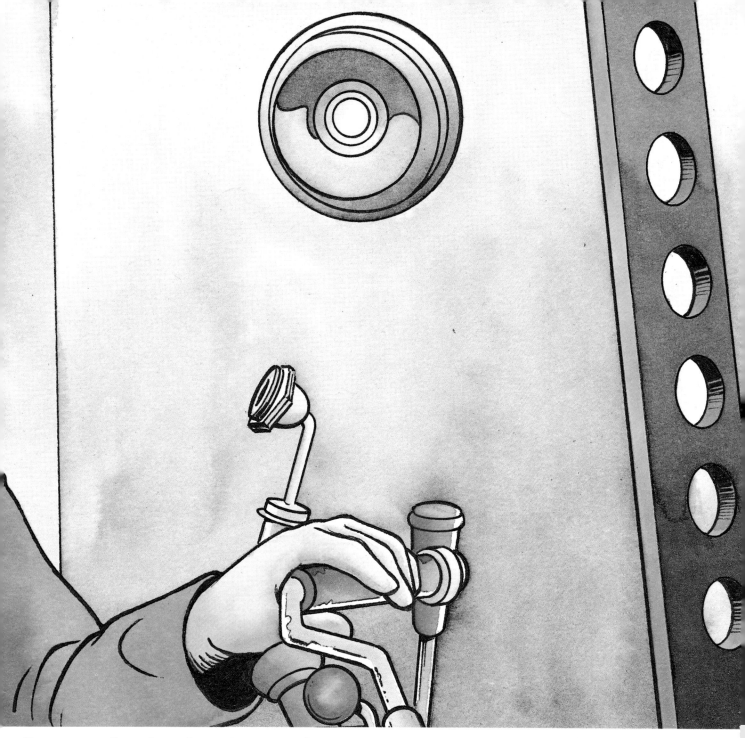

Scott radios back to base. 'Come in, Father, send Thunderbird 2 at once. We need the Mole.'

"OK, Scott. Virgil is on his way,' says Jeff.

The Mole is a big machine which can drill into rock. Thunderbird 2 will take the drilling machine to Windy Bay. The Mole is carried inside a big green pod.

Thunderbird 2 lands on top of the cliff.
'What's the problem, Scott?' asks Virgil.

'The boys are trapped in a cave at the bottom of the cliff. We must drill a tunnel to reach them,' says Scott.

Virgil unloads the Mole and begins to drill the tunnel.

When the tunnel is drilled, Scott climbs down into the cave. The boys are very happy to see him.

Scott straps a thick rope to each boy. 'Ready, Virgil,' he says, 'pull them up.'

'OK,' says Virgil and pulls the boys to safety.

Virgil and Scott have filled in the hole and it is time for them to leave.

'Next time,' Scott says, 'keep a lookout for the tide.'

'We will,' promise the boys, as they wave goodbye to their rescuers.